XERA THE SLAVE WOMAN

RASHMI NARSAPUR

Contents

1. Invasion Of The Southlands 1
2. The Rise Of The Sabbornese: 6
3. Xera,the Slave Woman 12
4. The Wrath Of The Crown Princess 14
5. The Druid's Mercy 16
6. Ancient Runes 19
7. The Dark Chant 22
8. The Preparations 25
9. The Invocation 27
10. The Temptress 32
11. The Beginning Of The End 33
12. Ivar, The Ruthless 35
13. The Golden Goddess 39
14. The Feast 42
15. The Massacre Of The Sabbornese 45
16. Lurin's Account 46
17. The Last Task 50
18. Baby Nuran 52
19. The Mother Goddess 55

CHAPTER ONE

Invasion of the SouthLands

They belonged to a harsh, icy, windswept land where hardly any vegetation grew. A thick layer of fog settled everywhere, making any movement impossible.

These icy lands wore a desolate look during the long, cold wintery months. The ground was covered with a thick frost save for a few shrubs that had managed to survive. These vegetation had only dried twigs from which long and drooping icicles hung.

These icy lands stood in a bowl of mountains that encircled them from all sides. The Myhak were the mountain ranges that seemed to reach the skies. Steep and snow covered, they offered little refuge to any life except for some mountain goats and birds like few jaegers and larks seen in brief periods of warmer climates.

But there were also the bears, big and brown and nightmare of all the land dwellers. They were vicious in nature and the scarcity of food had given an edge to their ferocity. True, their numbers were dwindling and the land dwellers had mastered the craft of attacking a bear in a group and killing it with the rudimentary weapons that they had fashioned out of stones and bones that they could lay their hands on.

Holding the little population that survived in the harsh climes in its captivity, the Myhak ranges offered little warmth. The melting snow during warmer periods formed rivulets which trickled down to form a myriad of lakes that dotted the icy lands. The small populace was thankful for this mercy of nature as it offered a rich harvest of fish that formed a major staple diet. Besides that, there was hardly any food to bring to the table save for the some quantity of grains grown on patches of soggy earth.

People who lived on this cruel land came to be known as Sabbornes. Opinions vary about this nomenclature but it is now accepted that the word Sabborn must have come from the word stubborn cause that is what they were.

Very fierce and independent, the Sabbornese seemed to possess a fiery will. This must have sprung from duelling with the cruelty of nature and living in its lap. But it had also given them the wisdom of acceptance and withdrawing when battles seemed hard to win. The Sabbornese had come to terms with the uncertainties of the nature, never knowing who will be claimed and when. The traps were too many to escape. There were the glaciers coming down from the Myhak's slopes and then there were the blizzards. A howling wind and a thick veil of billowing snow could trap and fling any hapless victim caught in its grip against huge rocks.

Then there was the thin ice which spread almost everywhere and was ever ready to gulp down an inexperienced person. And, then there were the bears that would spring from anywhere to make a fast meal of the terrified victim.

During the dark winter, people retreated into their longhouses built with wood and bones topped with a thatched roof. Here they sought shelter surviving on few grains which they had managed to grow on small patches of arable land during the brief periods of summer. Of course, the fish they had caught from the tiny lakes during the short respite of a summer and dried were a major additions to their meagre diet during the really harsh winters.

Still life went on. Though the Sabbornese had come to terms with the harsh realities of their lives and had carried on, there seemed to rise a silent anger and determination to change their fate.

These long drawn battles had made them edgy and cruel. With rolling years they grew impatient to move to warmer lands where nature was more gentle and generous; where its vagaries did not take a toll on their lives and where they could feed their little ones something more than the tasteless fish and soggy porridge. They yearned to get out of their cramped, dark dwellings to be able to breathe in fresh air and to feel the warm sun on their cold bodies.

The Sabbornese were tall and agile. Most possessed the sculpted body of an athletic build and chiselled features due to their life long duel with the harsh nature. They could withstand the deep winter with hunger in their bellies and determination in their eyes. They could run long distances, climb steep slopes of the Myhak and even swim in freezing waters of some lakes.

Some of the young men, then, had decided to move in packs to explore lands around to find out if conditions were better elsewhere. They had set out in different directions, promising each other that they would come back in some time bringing with them good tidings.

Some never returned; some lost their friends coming back broken and shaken. But there were a few who came back with much more than a promise. The news that they brought in was heart-warming. They spoke of lands in the south direction which were greener, warmer and safer! Moreover, they brought along with them a herd of magnificent animals, four-legged, tall and proud and called horses in the south lands. These animals, found in the wild could be tamed easily. They were fast runners. Intelligent creatures, they were also found to be loyal to their masters who caught them from the wild and trained them.

The acquisition of these animals who could also carry load had galvanised the Sabbornese plans to move to greener lands. Those who had seen these lands were full of good cheer and hope that these lands could deliver them from their omnipresent misery of cold, hunger and danger.

Once the decision was taken, plans were set into motion. Groups of young men, suitably clad with clothing and weapons left one fine morning. One group would bring back more horses and train them while other groups would explore these lands and get to know the locals.

Soon, as had been planned, a group returned with many horses, handsome in looks and ready to learn. They were tamed to take on a rider each along with some load. Further they were trained to ride still faster. Finally, they were trained to be part of the sword fight where their riders would indulge in a fake sword fight. Very soon, these horses, sharp creatures that they were, had learnt the art and craft of warfare and were edgy to take part in one.

In the meantime, the other groups which had gone on exploration, had discovered that the folks from the South Lands, as it came to be called, were peace loving and gentle in nature. They welcomed the northerners most willingly and even helped them out to settle. Their king, Magnus was loved by all. He was kind and generous and helped his subjects. The South Landers supported their king and almost worshiped him. The Trojans could see that it was a battle already won.

South Lands, were a picture in contrast to the harsh realities that the northern icy lands were. These lands were much warmer, greener and much more beautiful. Dotted with many lakes which had formed due to the regular rainfall, these lands also possessed large areas of cultivable lands. Many rivers formed by melting of the snow from the north provided a regular supply of water. The river banks and the vast adjoining areas, thus, were layered with a deep red soil made of rich fertile alluvial matter and a variety of crops were grown in it. This bounty of harvest had given the South Lands peace and prosperity and made its citizens friendly and happy. A society built on successful agriculture which yielded a bounty of harvest every season, the people had little to worry. Then, there was the Norj, the beautiful sea in the south. A vast, shimmering expanse of azure blue waters, Norj, not only offered the South Landers its rich vast coast to play and relax apart from an excellent opportunity to fish but also provided the protection from any invaders from south.

The only danger that could come was from the North. A fact, which this happy and relaxed population of the beautiful land never expected. Because for them, the North was nothing but a mighty range of snowy mountains where the ground was buried under the avalanches making the vast land barren. Any invasion from there was written off by the people whom the mercy of nature had made weaklings; a bitter realization which was to come much later.

CHAPTER TWO

The Rise of the Sabbornese:

The time, they say, is your friend or foe based on how you manage it. For the increasing population of the Sabbornese, who were moving in quietly in big numbers, the Time had not yet revealed its true intentions. But, the Sabbornese were a patient lot. Their lives in the desolately cold and barren icy lands had taught them the game of waiting and they could play it forever.

They were keen observers who were never given to anger. In a short time they had found out that the vast majority of the South Landers were a quiet and peace loving lot; a population which had never learnt the craft of a warfare. Their weaponry, too, was very poor and inadequate to deal with any onslaught. It was clear to the Sabbornese that their hosts not only despised a war but were actually afraid of one.

In the history of mankind, fear has been the most efficient weapon. With little to spend, it discharges its duty smoothly. The Sabbornese decided to use this fact to their advantage. As usual, they planned in detail and executed their plan with perfection.

To begin with, they began making friends with the locals. It was much easier than they had thought due to their gift of the gab and their very attractive looks.

In addition, the Sabbornese were a gifted community. Skilled in various arts, which their duelling with the harsh nature had taught them, they were extremely hard working, too. The South Landers were charmed beyond measure by these very helpful, hardworking people who were ever willing to lend a helping hand. They came across as a fearless lot who jumped in when trouble seemed to be brewing on a distant horizon. What was most impressive was, that their help came absolutely free of cost. These the Northerners appeared to be just content in helping. Little wonder that they soon became popular, gaining trust wherever they went.

This tactic, opened the doors of the wealthy South Landers who were close to the Royalty. Soon, invitations began to drop in from the high and mighty for the friendly Northerners who gladly accepted them.

Invitations came for various occasions. From weddings to christenings, from harvest festivities to fishing expeditions the invitations poured in from the Royals of the South Landers and the feudal lords, from the rich merchants and famous artists. Everyone wanted these charmers at their celebrations to make a grand success of their gatherings. All knew that these the Northerners could not only sing and dance or cook delicious meals but could also protect their friends should the situation arise. Though such was never a case, it gave an assurance of safety for the South Landers, an assurance which would soon turn fatal.

It was not long before that these charming community established a web of contacts among the South Landers. Offering help for the tiniest problem, they soon became indispensable. They would often be consulted on matters small and big. On matters of food and drinks, on matters of weather and travel. On matters of money and safety.

The Northerners would not only give advice but help to implement it. They were a patient lot and slowly but surely they spread their web.

In due course, they came to know many things, too many things, indeed. Details of the Royal family, their friends, their strengths, their weaknesses, their residences and their wealth. The Northerners came to know of the Royals' weaponry, their battle tactics and their army. But most importantly, they came to know of their mind set; their apathy towards their freedom and their complete lack of interest in guarding it.

A significant development had also been of arrangement of the Sabbornese in a hierarchical group. Over a period of time, they had realised that they worked best when they had a leader to respond to. Consequently, the Sabbornese had found themselves in the classic pattern of monarchy, which the history has shown to have its own strengths and follies.

The guy who had risen to the top was Ivar, a monster of a man whose absolute narcissism and intense ambitions cloaked in inhuman cruelty had pushed the Sabbornese to the high echelons of power.

And, so it came to pass. Under the single-minded leadership of Ivar, it was an easy road for the North landers; a downhill slide for the South Landers. They never knew how swiftly their friends from the North had begun to take interest in their political discussions and had begun to advice in the beginning but had later switched to dictating terms on their safety and freedom. The lenient taxes levied by the generous king were soon replaced by heavy taxes and a cruel imposition of paying them followed by heavy fines or punishments if payments did not come in time.

Still, the majority of the South Landers and the Royals themselves, believed that the Northerners were doing all this for their own good. That the Northerners were bringing change for the betterment of the South Landers. How naïve were they because they knew not that they, the South Landers, were digging their own graves slowly in the beginning but rapidly as time went by.

A few who could sense what was going on tried to raise an alarm; tried to warn the king. But it was a lost cause. The Royals were hypnotised by the convincing prowess of the charming the Northerners.

The few countrymen loyal to the Royalty, began to disappear one by one and stories of their ghastly death spread a fear in the remaining populace which watched in mute horror and a supressed acceptance of their fall from the grace.

Those few who had their wits about, began to make their escape plans, succeeding in the beginning as they fled by the sea route to distant lands. But later, as the Northerners came to know of this, the noose was tightened and these innocent subjects were caught and made prisoners. Some were killed off, the others made slaves in their own land, in front of their own people and in front of their own King.

King Magnus, generous and kind to a fault, though forgiving in nature began to sense that something was amiss. He could sense the silent plea in his subject's eyes. The mysterious disappearances and the consequent findings of the mutilated bodies of his friends and subjects made him restless. He realised that he could no longer trust the charmers from the North. He began to make plans to get together his people and his army to push off the intruders back to the North.

But his realisation had come too late. He had, in trusting total strangers, committed the single most mistake and now his countrymen were going to pay for it.

Drowned in guilt and self-loathing, he made the second big mistake of calling his army to wage a war against the people whom he had trusted. Too late, he realised that his own army had been quietly taken over by the very people who had assured him of their whole hearted support and complete safety.

The king was imprisoned and beheaded in front of all his subjects, the vast sea of mourners who watched this heinous crime with tear rimmed eyes. They all knew that their days of freedom and peace were over and the dark chapter of slavery had begun in their lives.

Within days, their beautiful homes were taken away by the very same people whom the South Landers had entertained with warmth and affection in their hearts. The once rich and talented lot found themselves on their own streets with nothing except the clothes on their back. But, the saga of their humiliation was far from over; in fact, it had just begun. Their friends from the North began to show their true colours when the soldiers of the North pushed these innocent and hapless victims out of the city limits of their own beautiful city. They were thrown away with contempt and were declared slaves of the Northerners.

Slaves! Many of the elderly South Landers wept openly and blamed their own lot and their king who had brought on such hardships on them. But they had failed to realise that in the human history, this had been an oft repeated chapter of treachery and betrayal from the very people whom one had trusted the most. The grief-stricken South

Landers could not understand that there was nothing called true friendship and all the relations were simply need based.

The lives of the South Landers went a sea change within a few days. Made to get up at the crack of dawn, they were subjected to a slew of arduous task which they, themselves as masters had never even asked their own paid servants to do. Along with the lowly beasts of burdens of all sorts, they were made to work on fields to grow crops for their masters. At the harvest, all the produce was snatched away from them, in return receiving just a few grains of the most inferior type.

They were made to work as masons and carpenters and painters and gardeners building beautiful homes next to their own beautiful homes. Those among them who were especially skilled were sought out and subjected to even harsher conditions to transform their own city, Southerna, which they had built with love and pride over generations. In front of their own eyes, they saw 'Southerna' being transformed into a monstrous citadel full of hideous buildings and now called 'Sabborna'.

The South Landers, turned into slaves, were pushed out of the city-limits of 'Sabborna' into a ghetto where they had to build hutments to protect their fragile bodies from the elements of nature. They had to rely on whatever scrap they could lay their hands on to build shabby dwellings where they brought their beaten spirits at the end of the each day, exhausted beyond measure. They cried themselves to sleep with hunger in their bellies and curses on their lips. Little did they know that the curses of a betrayed soul had the immense power to burn down a kingdom.

Only time would prove it.

CHAPTER THREE

Xera,the Slave Woman

Born to slave parents, who, just a few years ago were hardworking farmers proud of their farmlands in South Lands, Xera spent her early years with her parents, blissfully unaware of the harsh realities. She was taken away, one day when the Queen Mother's eyes fell on this pretty child. At the age of five, Xera was brutally snatched away by the palace guards to be a toy to the royal children. Her parents shed tears of blood. Would their anguish know no bounds?

An intelligent child that she was, Xera woke up to the inhuman reality and learnt ways to cope with it. She befriended a select few of the royal children, learning instinctively to keep away from other trouble makers. She learnt the subtle art of trading information for favours. Very soon, she became a favourite of most royal ladies with her ever helpful persona and cheerful banter. Gaining their trust, she was permitted to roam all over the palace but not step out of it.

Years passed and Xera grew into a beautiful young woman. Eyed with lust, she fell prey to most royal men of all ages. Her miseries became painfully shameful due to the pregnancies she had to hide and the abortions she had to endure.

Still, Xera carried on in a content manner as she knew there was no escape route. The children she grew up with, grew and got married having their own children. Xera learnt the most difficult art of seeing her own children, who were murdered in her womb, in these royal litters.

Years merged into decades and soon Xera was cradling the fourth generation princes in her lap. She got attached to little Krin, who would be the crown prince one day.

CHAPTER FOUR

The Wrath of the Crown Princess

Krinnea, the beautiful wife of the crown prince, Krin was an incorrigible devil in a human form. Arrogantly proud of her angelic looks, she spared no one and was especially cruel with the slaves. It was Krinnea's favourite past time to torture the poor souls making them beg for mercy. She had witnessed the special status that Xera had in the Royal household and was extremely resentful of it. She waited anxiously to find that one single opportunity to punish Xera and banish her to hell. She had even decided the punishment for Xera. The Vultures! Any commoner, let alone a slave simply wilted at the mention of that word. The most torturous and most painful punishment which was discovered by the Sabbornese and reserved for the traitors of the land was to throw the hapless victim into a field which was a sanctuary for those ugly birds. Once the poor soul landed on the ground, the vultures would swoop down and start tearing his flesh even as he was alive. His wails would be heard all over the land and people would pray for his early death.

Xera, though now old in body still possessed sharp sense and she knew that her days were numbered. She looked back at the time she had spent in the huge palace serving the four generations of the Sabbornese. She had no idea what had happened to her own family, her parents or her younger brother, whose fond memories were all that she had. She knew that the masters she served were evil and she had escaped their displeasure just by her wit and some abundant luck. She knew that the young crown princess eyed her cruelly and she shuddered at the thought of her wit being of little match against this Machiavellian woman.

Xera was frail now, a stooped toothless figure in dreary robes worn by generations of slaves. Her eyesight was dim and she could barely hear. Her evry limb ached and longed to rest, yet she would drag her burning soles doing some or other odd task lest she be noticed as a worthless chit of flesh.

That day had dawned as an unusually bright and Xera was ordered to bring a goblet of fresh juice from the palace kitchen. Putting one painful step after the other, she had managed to reach the magnificent chamber where the princess had reclined on a bed. Cradling her baby bump, she was lost in her reverie when Xera, gasping for breath, had brought her the drink. Trying to bow down at the same time offer the drink in a most polite manner, Xera had lost her balance and the drink had spilled on the princess's expensive gown. One look at the princess and Xera knew that she had lost her battle forever. As though in slow motion, the princess had got up jubilant at the opportunity that the fate had offered her. 'You are trying to kill my baby!' she had screamed through a hoarse voice and had ran to sound the gong that would bring the palace guards to the chamber.

CHAPTER FIVE

The Druid's Mercy

Mercifully, Xera did not remember much; of the searing pain, of the deep lacerations in her flesh made by the hungry, swooping vultures, of her deep humiliation by the very people whom she had served devotedly but who stood sneering and jeering as she was carried away by the soldiers to the Vultures' pit. There was no recollection of any of those horrifying moments which she spent facing death. All she could remember was the deep prayer as she called for her deliverance from the bondage. Her mind had blocked out all the bodily sensations. It was as though Xera was a in a trance, watching her body being torn apart by the screaming, hissing vultures. She almost stood aside as the blood poured out from the gaping holes. She marveled at this hapless creature who lay motionless, so unlike other pathetic victims who had tried to fight off, run away from those evil creatures who had finally carried away the mauled body.

It was her utter lack of resistance that saved her form the vultures. They were confused, looking down at the corpselike body which lay in a disgusting pool of blood. They tried to take out flesh from the ragged, shriveled body and decided that it was not juicy like other bodies thrown in the pit. They circled her and sat away.

Then they saw a human figure racing down at them with a flaming torch, the only thing that the vultures were scared of. They took off in the sky, disappointed at the feast served to them.

Druid Randolph was a well-known figure in the Sabbornese Kingdom. Well respected and even feared for his deep knowledge of the ancient mystic, Randolph was often consulted for matters of the mystic. He was treated differently, almost with a grudging reverence as the Sabbornese felt that questioning his authority of the mystic would be tantamount to invoking the Super Natural. Consequently, he was granted much freedom of space and action, much to the chagrin of some of the Royals.

His hermitage, a spacious expanse of the majestic trees and plants and bushes of various hues, was situated at the foothills of the Myhak Mountains. Hidden behind a fold of the foothills, the hermitage enjoyed a security that was extremely vital. With the strategic position of the Myhak Ranges, it was virtually impossible for the outsiders to find this place.

The lands of the hermitage had been generously gifted to the druid by the grateful Royals of the South Lands who were later massacred by the Sabbornese in the bloody battles. These lands of the hermitage were cultivated with much affection and care by the druid and a luxuriant hermitage stood proudly with spacious chambers for different activities.

Much work went on about the therapeutic properties of various extracts of roots and tubers and flowers. An army of disciples worked under the druid's sharp eye learning the crafts of making concoctions and the art of healing the patients. There was a huge, well stocked library of ancient books that was housed in a giant chamber.

When the blood dripping body of Xera was brought in by Randolph, the druid, his disciples and the healers gathered quickly around her to treat her deep wounds and bandage them. Most of them were horrified to see the terrible cuts made by the savage creatures. Even though the healers shuddered inwardly, they hid their feelings and tended to this frail old woman with utmost compassion. She was given different brews to sooth the burning wounds. A selection of fruits and flowers and juices was also given to her to help her gather her strength.

Xera lay quietly. She seemed to be sleeping, most of the times though Randolph knew differently. He knew that a very alert and ticking mind lay under that bandaged body and he wondered when she would be ready to fight back.

CHAPTER SIX

Ancient Runes

On a bright morning when sunlight was streaming through the big expanse of the windows, Randolph walked in the healing chambers only to find Xera's bed empty. Startled, he ran out calling her name. His disciples and healers heard his calls and rushed after him. The search party moved through the chamber after chamber but there was no sign of her. They then entered the verdant gardens and orchids laden with perfumed fruit n flowers. But the wounded lady was nowhere to be seen. They were frantic and grew sick with worries lest their patient was kidnapped away by the mighty Sabbornes. Though there was little to worry on that account cause for the Royals of the Sabbornese, the slaves and servants were little more than dust.

In the end when the druid and his search party were on the verge of giving up, Randolph remembered that he had mentioned the library to one of his disciples when he had sat next to Xera as she lay curled up lost to the world. Could she have heard him? But it made no sense. This had happened within couple of days of Xera being brought in. She was burning with fever then and blood and pus was pouring out through her wounds. Any mortal in the grip of those crushing pain would not have been able to pay attention to anything around him. The victim would have been buried in pain, begging for death. On an impulse, Randolph, the druid hurried to the library. As always, when he entered the hallowed cavernous chambers with vaulted ceilings, a calm descended over him. He had always wondered about this. Did the ancient books and manuscripts which he had so painstakingly collected from every corner of the world he had visited, induce a hypnotic charm? Was there a subtle magic that the books released that he was unaware of? He was not sure but he was certainly grateful for that. Many a times his troubled mind had brought him here and he had found peace even though the solutions to his problems were not yet visible. Today, too, he felt at peace when he began his search in the chambers of the library.

The library was a massive affair with chambers upon chambers built to accommodate the sheer volume of the books which Randolph had brought in. Many were gifted by his grateful patients whom he had liberated from the anguish of torturous bouts of pain and in certain cases from definite death. It had taken an army of his healers to sift through and categorise all the books and compile them and house them in different chambers of the sprawling library.

Now Randolph moved swiftly through the arches of its vaulted environs, his eyes searching for the frail lady. He knew that she could not have gone far, given her fragile health. Her wounds had just started healing and he knew that it would take great efforts for her to move even small distances. Yet, with a mounting surety, which he could not explain, he knew that he would find Xera here.

His hunch was right. He found her in the ancient runes section bent over a tattered manuscript, her tired eyes squinting over a page. Randolph stood motionless watching her and marvelling at the fighting spirit that lay whimpering in that battered, old body. Just by glancing at the tattered book he knew its contents and with a jolt he realised what she must be reading. Should he bring her out of the trance she seemed to be enveloped in? He pondered over the thought and at length decided not to. After all, this was her war and she had every right to acquire her weaponry and polish it before she blew the trumpet to call out her enemy out in the open.

CHAPTER SEVEN

The Dark Chant

Randolph stood there for a long time looking at the frail woman who seemed to be lost in the pages she was staring at. Apparently, something had caught her attention and she was trying to decipher the secret meaning behind those ominous words. Whatever that she had accidently stumbled on, must have been too bewildering cause Xera seemed to be drowned in those pages. After quite a while, Randolph coughed gently to make her aware of his presence. The action seemed to have fallen on deaf ears. She was engrossed in the text and it did not matter what went around her.

Sensing this, Randolph moved gently towards her and touched her. Though she felt his touch, Xera did not look up immediately. She continued to look down at the ancient pages whose writing was quite difficult to read. Randolph's patience paid off after some time and Xera turned slowly. Randolph looked at her and was jolted by what he saw.

Her eyes did not bear a vacant expression as before. Instead, they appeared to be twin flames of a strange emotion. Randolph could not put a word to the impressions they carried. They were a strange mixture of absolute hatred and triumph. It was almost as though Xera had stumbled upon something monstrously huge that could afford her retribution.

Acutely aware that he was treading on dangerous grounds, Randolph approached Xera cautiously and tapped gently on her back. Xera looked up and gave a soft smile. He realized that it was not a smile of weak acceptance but a beginning of quiet confidence that hovered on her lips. He stole a quick glance at the words she seemed to be transfixed on and shuddered inwardly. Because, as feared by him earlier, they belonged to an ancient dark chant which once unleashed, could bring in forces of mammoth proportions that could destroy the mankind.

'Sire', he heard her whisper. This was the first time that he had heard her speak. Unlike what he had expected, her words were clear. He looked at her keenly to know what she was saying. Indicating the text she was looking at, Xera asked him in quiet yet confident tones, 'Is this what I think it is?' Randolph weighed his words before he spoke because he knew that the listener was the victim who had served her masters devotedly for a very long time before being thrown to vultures to die an agonizing death. Deciding that there was nothing to be gained by holding back the vital information from this god fearing soul, he nodded in affirmation. Xera continued to hold him in her unwavering gaze. In the end Randolph relented and began, 'These are chants, dear. Very dark, indeed. They have the power to grant a wish which a seeker can ask, provided.. .'

Randolph hesitated before he went on. He knew that he had to be absolutely sure before he proceeded to unveil the truth. He was acutely aware that Xera was watching him, her every nerve and sinew listening in. Randolph closed his eyes still not sure if wanted to go through this. But suddenly, a figure flashed in front of him; that of a bloodied and battered old lady, cruelly flung in front of a hungry pack of vultures; the flying figures screeching and pouncing on her at once. Randolph opened his eyes with a jolt and began,' They are called Satanic Chants cause it is only the dark lord, Satan, who can grant the seeker one wish provided the price asked is paid in full.' Upon hearing this Xera seemed to withdraw into a shell. Her lips moved inaudibly but Randolph could understand her desperation and knew the question she would ask. How could, an old slave hope to have a treasure to pay the dark lord? Watching her drowned in the desperation, Randolph nudged her gently and whispered, 'The dark Lord, Satan does not seek any treasure. He seeks a promise, a commitment from the seeker. A promise that is almost impossible to honour. A seeker must understand that.'

It was as though a magic spell was cast. Xera eyes shone briefly before she closed them. 'Is it really that simple?' Her question was uttered in a quivering voice, disbelief dripping from it. 'No!' She heard Randolph say with a finality.

' There is something more. The seeker must chant without a single break, He must search out the dark lord and never stop chanting the chant till the Satan appears in front of him.'

Randolph watched Xera as she relaxed and turned around slowly. But Randolph was startled to see the beginning of a soft smile hover on her lips.

CHAPTER EIGHT

The Preparations

From that day onwards a change seemed to have come over Xera. If she had steadfastly ignored food earlier, she began eating; nibbling at her food first, progressing within a few days to eating well, gulping down big morsels of food. There was a spring in her steps as her walk went from a painful limp to a haltering shuffle to a confident stride. Her whole persona seemed to be changing. She dressed well choosing carefully from an assortments of garments offered by the healers; preferring warmer and loose fitting clothing that would give more freedom of movement. Her expression bore a veiled radiance as though she was humming a song which only she could hear. Only her eyes could betray the rage which she had hidden deeply.

Twice she had sought out Randolph after their fateful meeting in the library. She had probed deeply asking specific questions about the Chants. Randolph had asked her to remember the Chant thoroughly as she could never stop chanting once she began; a feat impossible to a mere mortal but she had accepted the condition readily. She was also told that she would have to go across the steep and craggy folds of the Myhak Mountains in search of the Dark Lord; another impossible feat for the ordinary folks but Xera was prepared for it. From the time she could remember as a small child, she had climbed the fierce mountain ranges on her feet while her little Royal Masters were carried in carved palanquins. Xera had not minded the torturous climb as she seemed to breathe in a fresh lease of life as long as she was out of the palace and in the laps of the mountain. She giggled merrily as Randolph tried to caution her about the near-freezing environment.

When nothing appeared to hold her back, Randolph stopped worrying and gave his whole hearted blessings. He knew that the pain in her heart was much greater than any fear.

The day before she left, Randolph paid her a visit to make sure that she had understood her mission. Except for a couple of close confidants, nobody had a clue about the superhuman challenge that the frail and shriveled old lady had accepted. It would have been ridiculous to even think that any young person could attempt to undertake such a bewildering task which could test his physical and mental reserves to a stretching limit let alone an old and battered woman.

But a few words with Xera and Randolph knew that for her, the call of her soul was impossible to ignore.

CHAPTER NINE

The Invocation

Oblivious to the intense pain that shot through her every nerve as she limped on blood spattered soles through the dark and deep jungles that lay at the foothills of the massive, craggy mountains, Xera carried on. Her tears had dried long ago as had the blood that had spilled through her red rimmed hollow eyes. Scanning every minute corner of the land that lay around her, her lips moved uttering an ancient chant that seemed to rise from those massive rocks which threatened to fall off the edges. She dragged her tiny wrinkled stooped body only on an immortal will. How else could you explain the strength that blazed through those eye which had seen no sleep in weeks or even months? How else could you not look at the gnarled feet that found the strength to bear the weight of her age ravaged body and not be surprised?

She paused not because she was tired but because she had come to the edge of the dark forests and looked up at the steep rocks that went up to the skies. Taking small shallow breaths that shook her frail body, Xera carried on. She had done this for a long time losing the count of weeks and months. Her only fear was of the Death and she knew that she had to do this before it claimed her. Putting one faltering foot after other she began the steep climb that would ultimately take her to her mission.

At the peak, Xera stopped and seemed to see her surroundings for the first time. Though not actually surprised but aware of the vast landscape for the first time, Xera went down on her shaky knees, her hands going up simultaneously. Bowing deeply she closed her eyes and continued the chant in earnest.

No words came out and the wind kept count of the passing minutes. The ancient rocks looked on and Xera prayed. Soon the winds picked up strength moving in circles creating a powerful vortex. It was a miracle that the old lady still managed to stay on the ground her head bent in an unknown prayer.

The day melted into a dark night which watched the old warrior's lone battle. An intense cold enveloped the mountains and the deep valleys, leaving a bluish frost on the bare branches. Xera's bony structure was now covered with a layer of frost through which a small movement of her lips could hardly be seen. The night's vigil ended as a feeble sun cast few rays. The birds hid in the snow covered branches afraid to come out. The water had long ago frozen in icicles that watched the old lady's silent march. Then, all of a sudden a strong wind swept through the mountains howling as it went. It circled the bluish figure and hovered around. Still Xera continued her slow fight with a hunger, refusing to look up.

''What do you wish for?' thundered a deep voice and then Xera looked up through eyes that had almost lost their vision. She could hardly see the dark figure that towered over her. 'Speak on, Woman!' came the command and Xera struggled to her feet. As her lips moved her raspy breath formed a small icy cloud but He heard no words. 'Name your wish!' said He. They were words uttered in command

and cloaked in contempt. But He knew that the power of those gasping words that chanted the Mantra could chain Him to this weakling of a woman forever.

Did Xera know? Perhaps she knew, perhaps not. But she was beyond caring. She looked up and said, 'I pray for...'and then her body was consumed by a strong bout of cough that shook her violently. The dark figure stood impatiently waiting for her to recover. Gasping for breath Xera opened her mouth and whispered, 'I pray for....'. She stopped and peered through the haze to take in the giant figure standing so majestically. 'I shall not wait till eternity to hear your Prayers' thundered the figure. But He did not vanish.

It was then that a small smile hovered on Xera's wrinkled face. Gathering her strength she began now, clear in the knowledge and her intentions, 'I pray for the eternal youth and beauty!' But even before her words were completely out, she heard a loud raucous roar of an ugly laughter.

'Are you insane, woman?' she heard Him say. But she was ready now, firm in her knowledge, sure of her power. 'I pray for the eternal youth and beauty, My Lord' she said softly. They were the words of steel which held the minutest chill detectable. As the towering presence looked on, Xera went down on her knees and began a monologue that came from her shrunken black lips which covered her thin teeth less mouth. 'Make me the most beautiful woman, the most desired woman on earth. Let there be no man whose heart is not put on flame and whose mind does not go blank when he sees me. Make me the ultimate temptress who can destroy the wills of men and put their honour in a bondage. I seek this from you, My Lord!' And then she stopped suddenly.

There were no words now, no taunts, and no raucous laughter. Only a chilly silence.

And then the towering Figure spoke, 'And what can you offer me?' Even though his words were softer, the contempt was all there but it was guarded now. Xera seemed to be silent for a while. But when she looked up, she was firmer and the words that came out showed a strength which did not match the frail body. 'I offer my soul, My Lord!' Said the old woman who sat stooped and hunched. 'My soul which is as pure as a child's laughter, as pure as the waters of a brook. My soul, which had till now known no hatred, no jealousy, and no enmity. Grant me my wish and take away my soul, My Lord! I have no use for it.' She waited, still stooped but not shaking; sure in her power of her mind, sure in power of her offering. The silence that oozed from everywhere persisted like a thick fog as the towering presence stood motionless for a while. Ultimately it relented and said in a softer tone, 'Very well, then! You will be the most beautiful woman who will be eternally young. There will be no man who will be able to fight your charms. Wars will be fought and men will become slaves of your charm. Kingdoms will be destroyed and Heavens will fall at your knees but.....'And He stopped suddenly.

Xera's head came up now, 'But what, My Lord?' said she in a whisper. And it is said that the words that followed had the wisdom of the ages written in them. The words whose contents could shake the heavens, for the price asked for, was far too great, for mortals and the immortals, alike. 'You, Xera, shall never be allowed to love anyone. The gift of love shall be denied to you, forever. The magic of your beauty shall be taken away if..

Xera's head went down only for the minutest of a fraction but when it came up her eyes blazed with an intensity. 'I accept, My Lord!' she said simply and the figure melted away. Xera got to her feet slowly but sure in the knowledge that a new dawn was breaking.

The mountains and the brooks and the trees and the bushes had the faintest impression of a ray of golden sun and of a silver moon that had melted together and had moved away in a grace that had never been seen earlier. With their collective wisdom they had realised that the beginning of the end had begun.

They stood in witness as they had from time immemorial and sighed in deep grief.

CHAPTER TEN

The Temptress

Erik rode out of the palace as the first rays of the sun streamed into the courtyard. He loved to mount his steed that galloped into the deep forests on the foothills of Myhak Mountains with the wind in his golden curls. Unlike his elder brother Krin, the crown prince, Erik loved the outdoors and spent as much time as he could in the green-blue woods, on the slopes of rocky black mountain and by the silver beaches of Norj, the azure blue sea that lined the Sabbornese kingdom. He enjoyed driving Leif, his dependable steed into the oncoming waves of Norj and both of them would enjoy a huge splash in the waves.

That day was no different; except that it changed his life forever. As Leif galloped closer to the foothills of Myhak Mountains, his master got ready to face the fast upward climb that lay in their path. Just before Leif began the steep climb, he suddenly reared his front legs almost toppling his master. Erik was about to kick his steed in rage when he had an acute sensation of being watched by somebody. He turned left to see what it was that had caught Leif off guard and looked into the deepest of the blue eyes. Erik thought he was looking at the molten sunshine when she smiled mysteriously. As he stood motionless, she came near and said in a husky tone, 'I am Rays. Will you take me home?'

CHAPTER ELEVEN

The Beginning of the End

Erik lost all sense of time. He had no idea how he had carried this golden beauty home. He felt that he was lifting a ball of woven silk when he had scooped her up in his arms and had carried away. She smelt like a garden in spring bursting with a thousand fragrances. Her gentle laughter was akin to a gurgle of a small brook. And her mane of gold was what fantasies were made of.

On his way back to his palace, he was aware of the curious eyes looking up at this beautiful creature in his arms. But they seemed to be falling in a trance as soon as they had rested on her. They were hypnotized by her ethereal beauty. Some people even gasped loudly as they stared at her. And Erik glowed in sheer pride. After all, she had chosen to come home with him! He would have been devastated to know that he had carried home a golden torch instead of a silky body.

Their days and nights were spent in sheer rapture. Rays knew a thousand ways to please him. She could cook a gamut of dishes to appeal to his taste buds. She would sing hundreds of songs in her lilting voice. She would dance in a most carefree way and her postures were most erotic. In bed, she was a like volcano erupting into splendorous hot lava and satiating her prince in thousands of timeless ways. Erik felt that he was the Emperor of the Heaven; till he ran into his father; the Great King Ivar of the Sabbornese.

CHAPTER TWELVE

Ivar, the Ruthless

He was not called ruthless for nothing. Ivar, the giant among giants was the ruler who had contributed to The Great Sabbornese reign with the cruelest efficiency. Both his subjects and enemies quaked in fear upon hearing his name and would rather kill themselves than be subjected to his tyranny. He had a monstrous ambition for his race and insatiable lust for women. His heart was like a rock, totally devoid of any feelings except for his two sons; crown prince Krin and his younger brother Erik. Both born to the two lovely sisters Amaya and Amaha, the boys were looked after by an army of servants after their mothers had thrown themselves from the peaks of Myhak Mountains, preferring certain death to the cruel and unnatural lust of Ivar.

Ivar adored the boys and made certain that they received the best of the care and education to be fit to be Royalties. He always spent some time with both his sons and taught them the war skills which they would require. His heart would be filled with pride when he looked at his two blond sons.

On that fateful day, when he had not heard from his son Erik for a few days, Ivar, the ruthless decided to pay Erik a visit and so had come to his palace. The soldiers guarding the palace bowed deeply. Ivar strode through the lovely gardens trampling the flower beds and calling out his son's name. His eyes wandered over the palace and the gardens looking for him. He remembered that this palace was specially built for Erik after his mother Amaha had died so tragically. Why would anyone want to throw oneself from a very steep craggy surface? Knowing fully well that instant death waited with her jaws open wide? Ivar did feel pity for the young mother who was not allowed to see her newborn infant before she had danced naked in front of Ivar and his drunk friends. She could have chosen any of the Royals who were present that night baying lustily. Poor thing. But, her death, which was followed by the death of her sister Amaya had indeed come as a rude shock and for a few nights Ivar had felt restless. Finally, he had come up with a solution to the haunting images of their bodies, torn into thousands of pieces, as they were recovered from the deep ravines below the Myhak Mountains.

He had decided to build the most luxurious palace for his second born. Many courtiers had gently tried to remind him that it would be unwise to do so as the second prince Erik would not be the crown prince. But all the reminders had fallen on deaf ears and a beautiful and majestic palace had come up. Ultimately both the princes had been moved to King Ivar's main palace. It was only in recent years, after the Crown Prince Krin had married the beautiful princess from Kaloha islands and named her Krinnea that Erik had moved to this beautiful palace which lay vacant all these years, Ivar rarely paying a visit to it.

All the past came rushing to Ivar as he headed towards the main entrance. He could hear his second born speak to someone. It was unusual because Erik's voice seemed so different as though drunk on joy. Erik was calling out to someone. Ivar stood motionless for some time. Who was he speaking to? He had never heard Erik being so happy. Who was responsible for it? He did not have to wait. He heard running footsteps and saw Rays coming out in the garden.

An initial impression of her was that of a giggle bearing a human body. A mass of tangled gold for her hair and a lithe body in race was all he could see. But slowly her face was visible and Ivar was totally jolted out of his wit. Here was a female form carved out in sheer perfection. From her large luminous eyes, her petit nose, her full mouth which promised ecstatic pleasure to her suitor to her voluptuous breasts to her slender waist and her well rounded hips was a magic of absolute perfection. And then their eyes met and Rays gave him her most dazzling smile.

Ivar stood rooted to the ground his heart pounding wildly. He took in her most erotic body and he felt an ache shoot through his loins. He could not share this treasure with anyone; not even his son.

Just then Erik came out calling out to her. But one look at his father and the entire sequence of forthcoming events cascaded in front of him. No! He would not hand over this exquisite angel to anyone, not even to his father.

That was his last living thought before he was struck by Ivar, the cruel's sword. In no time, Erik's body was lying in a pool of blood, his head cut off and thrown in a trampled flowerbed.

Rays stood there taking in all the events. She looked down at Erik's headless body lying at her feet and a burning ache filled her heart. Erik! He was such a cute baby! Xera had often played with the infant, feeding him, cooing into his tiny ears that made him giggle. Many a times, she had held him till he slept, when as an infant he had clung to her, missing his mother. All the memories came flashing by but they could not help her. She pushed them away and looked up into the hungry eyes of Ivar. The King of the Sabbornese! She smiled at him beckoning the monster to her.

CHAPTER THIRTEEN

The Golden Goddess

The news of Erik's death spread like a wild fire throughout the kingdom and an ominous hush fell all over. The subjects and the slaves discussed this over lit fires in open fields. The soldiers sneered at the weakling of a prince envying the old king. Only one person was unaffected by this. 'She is on her way' said Randolph to himself closing the door behind him as one of his disciples had brought in the disturbing news.

And, so, it came to pass. Everyone was talking about Ivar's beautiful mistress. Wild rumors flew thick and strong. Some said that she had golden serpents coming out of her head hissing while others talked of golden wings and how she could fly on a dark night. There were talks of her petal smooth skin and her child like voice. It were only the elderly and the wise who had realized that this was somehow different, unnatural. The arrival of a golden goddess from nowhere spelt huge trouble for the Sabbornese. Those among the subjects and slaves, the tortured majority prayed that their hunch would turn out to be true; that She indeed was the deliverer who would release them from their bondage.

Every day brought in more gossip. Among the servants, there were discussions of how graciously kind this lady was who accepted any service with absolute sweetness. Nobody was allowed to look up at her, of course. With eyes down cast, they could only hear her childlike eager voice when they carried food inside. And perhaps, see the milky white skin of her ankles. But they all knew. They knew that just one glance up could cost them their life, just as it had cost Prince Erik.

She would thank them deeply. The soldiers could see her dance as the shadow of her agile body moved on the curtains. For slaves, she seemed an angel from heavens as the heinous killings of them had almost come to a standstill. Ivar was sobering down.

And, it was a welcome observation for all; from the ranks and files of the army, battle worn and weary to his ministers, sick and tired of Ivar's ever changing moods and commands; to his subjects and slaves a welcome change for all of them as they could breathe in a little easily aware that their monstrous king could change his mood anytime. They sent out prayers thanking the golden goddess.

But it was to change very soon.

The courtiers dressed in their absolute finery were sent out one day to all the powerful people of the kingdom. It included the Royals and Feudal lords, the rich merchants and the top jewelers, the famous artists and the skilled artisans of the city. Bursting with curiosity, they had opened the royal envelope bearing the palace insignia. The contents of the envelope drove their breaths away!

There was to be a huge gala on the night of the next full moon and everyone who was a Royal or rich was invited.

The Royal palace began to get a new look. Designers and Painters called in from all over the country scrubbed and painted the walls with shimmering hues. Curtains of exotic finery were hung from all the windows and doors.

Gardeners toiled in the red soil, cutting and pruning and shaping the plants into exotic shapes. On the eve of the gala the palace and the gardens were lit with thousands of twinkling lights giving it a fairy tale look.

The Royal kitchen was busy preparing an array of delicious food for the guests. There was an array of mouthwatering delicacies and their aroma wafted from the kitchen as the servants bustled around bringing a myriad of things for the Royal cooks.

Musicians had gathered in one corner of the vast gardens. They had brought in an orchestra of musical instruments which included the flutes, lyres, string instruments like harps, lures and drums. The strains of enchanting music began to fill up the gardens and the people were truly happy for the first time to witness these activities. Some of the elderly remembered the old rule under the king Magnus and wept openly. The Golden Goddess indeed had unleashed a miracle.

CHAPTER FOURTEEN

The Feast

The sun began its descent to the west as the guests started alighting from their coaches. It was a gathering of the Sabbornes' finest. There were the Royals, Ivar's close kin, his uncles and aunts, his cousins and his first born Krin with his lovely wife Krinnea. They all came out of fear for they knew about Erik's gruesome death and did not wish the same fate upon them.

Then there were the knights and feudal lords, who swore allegiance to the great king; a relation shaped by fear and disgust of the cruel king.

Then there were merchants and jewelers all steeped in money. All those who had gathered riches by cheating subjects of their hard earned money by winning favours from the king. They had brought in cheap goods from far off lands and had sold them in the markets of Sabbornes scaring off the local craftsmen; their cunning always backed by the Royal seal. Some of the dwindling numbers of artists and artisans had tried to flee the land unsuccessfully, being caught by the soldiers due to the Royal decree. These poor creatures had had to bear the wrath of the Royal cruelty. Some had committed suicide while the remaining had turned mute spectators to the greed and lust for power of these merchants.

But oppressors knew that the money meant nothing to Ivar. With one raised finger, he could crush anyone, siblings, subjects, soldiers alike.

The sun had cast its golden hues on the palace gardens as guests started mingling and speaking in hushed tones. They admired the grandeur, their faces reflecting the awe they felt. With its myriad lights and bouquets of flowers and the hypnotic strains of music the palace seemed to be enveloped in a magical aura. All eyes were now on the giant staircases that wound its way to the upper quarters.

Suddenly the music stopped playing only to begin in high pitched notes as all eyes swung to the top of the staircase. Standing right at the top in his full regalia was Ivar and on his arms was the most delicate and beautiful woman the mankind had ever known. Drunk on power and arrogance Ivar made his way down as Rays clung to him in adoration.

Every single eye was on the pair filled with rapture for Ray's beauty and jealousy for Ivar. It was a perfect combination of the Beauty and the Beast.

As they reached the grand hall, Rays reached out and kissed Ivar deeply drowning the majestic hall in a thunderous applause. Then she led him to the dance floor and began dancing gracefully. Ivar stumbled as he tried to keep pace with this golden creature who seemed to glide on the dance floor swaying to the gentle music in a hypnotic style. Then she turned around beckoning others to join them.

The guests looked with great trepidation at their master who nodded with a smile. Soon the floor was taken up by many couples dancing in the bewitching mood, the cruelty of the king forgiven.

Or was it?

For the soldiers outside who were guarding the palace gates, this evening came as a complete shock. They could not believe their cruel king turning into a gentle host. But they were happy as it meant some of that kindness was coming to them, too. It was a very cold night outside the palace gates and the soldiers busied themselves around the generous fires they had lit. They were sure in the knowledge that the night would be a great success and their task of security to the King and his guests would be a child's play.

How wrong were they!

CHAPTER FIFTEEN

The Massacre of the Sabbornese

The first of the screams pierced the velvety dark, cold night a little later after the merriment had begun. It was a blood curdling scream followed by many such screams. There were cries and groans coming from inside the majestic hall and the chief of the soldiers dashed inside. With their weapons drawn, many soldiers followed him. With lightning speed, they crossed the gardens and entered the hall. What they saw stopped them in tracks.

King Ivar stood in the middle of the hall his sword held high, blood dripping from it. Crown Prince Krin's beheaded body lay in a pool of blood at his feet along with many of the bodies which belonged to his loyal coterie. Some of the friends had drawn out their swords and were inching towards the King.

The chief of the soldiers took one look at this and forged ahead to save the king. Other soldiers followed him, all absolutely in dark as to what devilry had taken place.

CHAPTER SIXTEEN

Lurin's Account

Lurin trembled as he stood in front of the great druid. His instructions had been precise. He was to enter the palace through back gates as one of the kitchen helps and make way towards the majestic hall in an unobtrusive way. He was to hide behind one of the big curtains till the guests had arrived and then act as a water bearer. He had done all that and more.

Just before the sun had cast its last golden rays on the city, Lurin had not only managed to slip in the kitchen but had also befriended one of the kitchen helps. He had introduced himself as Torin, one of the many helps hired by the palace for the festivities. He, then had proceeded to observe his surroundings, making his way to the majestic hall as the great gong had sounded.

Knowing that it signaled the arrival of king Ivar, Lurin had slipped into the majestic hall and had hid himself behind the billowing curtains, making sure that he could observe the happenings of the majestic hall.

Within a few moments, he had seen king Ivar arrive with the most beautiful woman on his arm. Lurin, who prided on his knowledge of herbs and plants had had little interest in women and had treated the ones who were his family and friends with respect. He had never taken a woman nor found anyone worth his time or effort.

But one look at the angelic form resting ever so lightly on Ivar's arm, Lurin had felt his senses quicken. He felt instantly drawn to this golden beauty. He wanted to rush out and take her in his arms.

'Do not look at her, I repeat, do not look at her, cause you shall not come back alive' Randolph's warnings had rung clear and loud in his mind. Obeying those orders hastily but reluctantly he had withdrawn his glance from her. With a shock, He had realized that the lovely lady had had the same effect on all the men while the ladies assembled squirmed in jealousy and embarrassment. It was as though the lovely creature was casting a spell on all the men present. They seemed to be melting in her presence.

Careful not to look at this golden witch, Lurin began observing all the guests. He could identify many royalties, as they had been treated by his master on a number of occasions. Lurin, himself had treated many of these halfwits upon his master's instructions, accompanying Randolph to their palaces. He had sneered at their false bravado and their megalomania knowing that without the king's backing their lives would be reduced to nothing.

Today, he realized that, these jesters of the Royalty could be eliminated if they as much as looked up at the golden witch.

Lurin's predictions proved to be on mark as the events unfolded on that ominous evening. Now, standing before the great master and looking back on the bloodied accounts that took place in front of him, he shuddered as he began, 'I was there ,O Great Master!' 'I was there on the day when the strength of the men failed. I was there when they became helpless slaves to the silent charm of the golden witch. I watched as king Ivar brought her down and was kissed by her. Then she took him to the dance floor and began the most hypnotic dance that there could have been. All the guests stood staring at them; as though bound by a spell cause how else could you explain the helpless lust that all of them felt? They all looked as the sacrificial lambs waiting for their turn.

Then, the golden lady's eyes fell on Prince Krin and she gave a most dazzling smile. The entire hall seemed to be illuminated by that smile. Prince Krin stepped forward and took her in his arms. The pair moved away dancing to the music. Everyone was watching them with lust and hunger in their eyes. I felt ill at ease as though something really horrible was about to happen. That's when I looked at the king and my mouth went dry.' Lurin came to a halt gasping for breath.

'What did you see, Lurin?' Randolph prodded him gently. Lurin's eye wore a vacant expression. He seemed to be struggling with himself. Then, realizing that his master was watching him Lurin continued his tale. 'King Ivar was in a great rage. He had pulled out his sword and had followed prince Krin. The Crown prince was dancing with gay abandon. He did not realize that his life was about to end. In a swift movement, Ivar cut off his son's head and looked at his beheaded body in disgust.

As he swept his eyes over the gathering, most trembled from this hideous killing and moved back while a few pulled out their swords and charged towards the king. It was then the soldiers entered the hall and moved towards the king.

In no time, all hell broke loose. One could only see fountains of blood jetting out of the cut limbs and hear blood curdling screams from all over. I did not think I would be spared and stood rooted at the spot. The beautiful interiors were splattered with blood. The walls and the curtains and the furniture was blood soaked. I closed my eyes and prayed for a swift death.

Nothing happened for a while as time ticked away. Slowly I opened my eyes to see no one standing. There was a heap of mutilated bodies on the floor. No one was spared. All the guests including the women, servants, soldiers and slaves were massacred. The great king Ivar lay dead with his chest ripped open. Some of the musicians and cooks who had heard the commotion and had their wits around had managed to escape. My eyes moved around to see any movement in this utter madness when they fell on her. The golden lady was climbing up the stairs humming a tune as though nothing had happened.'

As Lurin stopped his account, a hush fell over in the library where he was summoned. He looked at Randolph expectedly who seemed to be lost in his thoughts. 'Master, any orders for me?' Lurin asked softly.

Still in deep thoughts, Randolph shook his head and whispered,'Xera has had her wish. I wonder what she will do now.' And without a word to his disciple, Randolph walked out of the library.

CHAPTER SEVENTEEN

The Last Task

A hush had fallen over the Royal palace. It was completely deserted. Not a soul was seen around. Nobody attempted to enter it. The news of the gruesome killings had spread around like a wild fire. A few survivors of the massacre had fled the kingdom lest they be brought back for a cruel interrogation. It was the time of quiet whispers and rumors that went around with the howling of jackals and whooping of hyenas entering the palace attracted by the strong odour of rotting flesh and blood.

No one had heard about the golden lady as Rays came to be called. Had she fled too or vanished in the thin air? The air around the palace hung around like damp, thick black soot.

Then, on the morning of the third day of the aftermath, a woodcutter's young son saw a miracle. He saw a young woman emerge out of the palace. His impression was of a white lily. Dressed in pure white robes, she seemed radiant and happy. He later recalled that there was not even a scratch on her body as she walked out, her head held high, humming a song softly. She seemed completely unaffected by the blood soaked walls or the heaps of dead bodies that lay rotting around. What was most intriguing was the fear seen in wild animals feasting on the dead bodies, as she was seen coming down the stairs. They retreated in fear as she walked casually swinging her well rounded hips as though to a market.

A little later, she emerged in the section that housed the commoners. She was watched quietly by hundreds of eyes. By now, the events of that violent night had been heard and discussed by all and the people had come to the conclusion that she was indeed a witch who could cast a hypnotic spell by just her smile or glance. Rays looked around this part of the city and remembered how she had carried heavy weights, too heavy for her thin, small young frame. She remembered how she was ordered around, pushed around, beaten harshly for tasks left incomplete by her for the little girl had no energy to do them on an empty stomach. She remembered how she had fainted many a times under strong sun and was ignored or kicked out of the way. Not a single person had brought her a morsel of food or a drop of water. Today, she could choose to drag each one of them out and lust after her and have them kill each other as she had done in the Royal palace. They all seemed too insignificant now like worms eating king Ivar's body. She had seen enough of this part of the city. She needed to visit another place before she could complete the last task.

Citizens of the city saw her stroll out of their area but dared not heave a sigh of relief. They had understood her power and had no wish to confront her. They watched her leave and prayed that she would never return.

CHAPTER EIGHTEEN

Baby Nuran

She was still humming that song which her mother would sing while cooking. She could remember it clearly as she had sung it many a times when she was hungry or beaten or raped and thrown out; somehow, her young mind had built a strong wall by humming the melody that gave her both strength and hope. Today she wanted to visit the source of her strength before she bid it a final adieu.

In a little while, she reached the outskirts of the city and could see the hutments in the distance. She could see them clearly as she came nearer. Of dried branches and twigs were they; of pieces of metal bars and stones they could scavenge after the Royals and the commoners had thrown out. The huts were small and smelt of rotten food, the only edibles that reached their part. There was very little of value there, torn and dirty clothes, broken toys and just a few mangled pots. There was dirt and squalor everywhere and desperation hung thick around. Nothing had changed. She seemed to go back in time. As she entered this area, the slaves recognized her. There were loud whispers and they disappeared in their huts.

She smiled to herself and moved on. She was looking for the little hut of her childhood in front of which she would play with her younger brother. Little Nuran was barely two year old. He was a sickly thin child who cried often. The food was never sufficient but she would make up for it by her little plays and laughter. She would carry him around showing different things while making small toys out of wet earth and leaves. Barely a few years older to him, she had learnt the art of mothering him and had proved to be an excellent mother when her own mother was called away for palace duties for days on end.

All the families lived in abject poverty and were tormented by the uncertainty of their lives. They never knew who would be picked by the palace guards but knew that most of them would never return. But little Xera neither knew this nor was ready for it. One day when she was playing with little Nuran, a chariot pulled out in front of them and out stepped a lady who was dressed in royal clothes and possessed a haughty demeanor. Much, much later, Xera had realized that this woman was the Queen Mother, a woman who was feared by all. She was accompanied by palace guards. She pointed at the little girl playing with a small child. Quickly, a palace guard stepped forward and pulled the startled little girl away. He carried her away. She had no time to even bid goodbye to her little brother who played on unnoticed.

Finally, she had been able to locate the place where her hut had stood many decades ago. There was no sign of it nor of the tree which stood behind her hut. She had lost her parents and her little brother a very long time ago. All she remembered was the tune she would hum to herself to bring a measure of comfort to her aching heart. Tears streaming down her eyes, she stood there for a long time before turning back abruptly and walking away.

Her steps back were quick and firm. She did not hum the song nor did she look around as she passed the desolate land. She had visited places which she wanted to. She was eager now to honor the one last task before she submitted herself. Gaining in speed, she walked quickly and soon reached the palace of the crown prince Krin.

She did not know what to expect as both the crown prince and his beautiful arrogant wife had been killed in the massacre. But she was not looking for them. She went in and found it to be quiet, too, though she could hear some movements and whispers. A slave came out hearing her footsteps but fled as soon as she saw Her. She now moved quickly inside. She knew where the nursery was, having spent lot of her time there getting it ready for the next prince.

The baby was exactly there where she had hoped him to be. A beautiful baby boy, only a few months old, was playing in the cradle. A bundle of soft cotton and a mass of golden curly hair, he was a miniature copy of his father, Prince Krin. He was cooing and gurgling. She lifted him as she had lifted his father in her arms and whispered something. The baby laughed out in pure joy; exactly as Nuran had laughed.

She continued to whisper in his ears as she gently caressed him. The baby seemed to enjoy it and giggled loudly.

As she turned to go, she realized that a few slaves had assembled with fear writ large on their faces. Was she a monster to them? She did not care. But as she began to move with the infant in her arms, the slaves flung themselves at her feet and begged for the child's life. They were sick with worry. Would they see the little one, ever? Or would it meet the same fate as that of his parents? They could not stop the golden witch as she glided on with baby Krin firmly in her arms.

CHAPTER NINETEEN

The Mother Goddess

It was a long walk to the hermitage and she knew that time was running out for all. By now, the news must have spread across neighboring countries and the kings there would be preparing to attack. She must not waste any more time, she told herself repeatedly. The only sanctuary she could hope to find was at the hermitage. She knew she would be welcome there anytime.

Would her hunch be right or would she be turned away from there, too?

She hurried to the hermitage. It was getting hot and the sun's fierce climb was making it extremely difficult for her to carry the child and reach the hermitage.

She reached the hermitage after a long time, gasping for breath but it was impossible for her to locate the entrance. Luckily, Lurin, as directed by Randolph, was waiting for her and she gratefully accepted his offer of assistance.

She was received by Randolph. The healers took away the little one to feed and clothe and to put to bed. She was now alone with the great druid and for the first time, she felt vulnerable and unsure. Tears stung her eyes as she relived the memories of the past few days. From her near death experience in the vulture pit to the massacre of the Sabbornese, it had been a huge weight of events and she suddenly felt very tired of this. But she was eager to finish her last task. What would the great druid say?

As though reading her mind, he said in a soft tone. 'You have come a long way, dear. You finished what you set out to do and that is a comforting thought. I suggest you rest before planning ahead.' She shook her head and said, 'We all know that attack from the other kings will be any day now. Though the hermitage will offer protection for some time, all of you will have to leave for safe pastures.'

'Ah, but you will come with us. We will not abandon you nor the baby.' Said Randolph reassuringly. She smiled before going on, 'Yes, I have no doubt about it. But, my time here is over, Oh Great Master. My ship has sailed and I must leave. I do not have the strength or the desire to continue this wretched life. I look for liberation, my lord!'

And Randolph understood. He understood her pain, her desire to leave and her desire to finish her responsibility of the events which she had begun.' Very well, then, Xera! You must do what your soul wants.'

Hearing her name, she smiled and got up to her feet. She kissed Randolph's hands and said her prayers. But before she could go on, Randolph stopped her and said, 'I ask you to wait for just a few day and reconsider your decision. If you continue to feel the same way, I shall not stop you.'

Hiding her disappointment, Xera left for her quarters as Randolph sat back to think. He had a lot to plan. It had crossed his mind earlier that soon there could be an attack by outsiders but with Xera's voicing the same concern he had understood the enormity of it. He had understood that the hermitage would not offer them the security should the attack come by a strong foe. He would have to move with his disciples and his books. And that would need great planning. Randolph was indeed glad that he had already set into motion a number of steps to ensure this.

The dawn of the next morning broke very early for Randolph who had been up in his study from the wee hours and was planning the steps for a successful escape, should the need arise. He had already sent some of his most resourceful disciples in the guise of commoners to look for any trouble. He knew he would have to organize groups to pack and load books as well as some of the stock of medicines so they could move fast. And now, there was Xera and the baby. As Ray, she could be recognized and hounded everywhere; as Xera, she would have neither the energy nor the will. Fleeing with a small infant, especially one who was a born Royal could pose a whole set of problems. With a deep sigh Randolph wished that none of this had come to him. That he would have been left undisturbed to carry on the work he loved the most; the work of healing people and to work on newer medicines to make the healing quicker and smoother. But he realized that it was not up to him to wish. What was given to him was the time to do what he could do. And, that's precisely what he had set out to do.

The next morning rose with a warmth and cheer that brought smiles to everyone in the hermitage. They had forgotten what the magic of a baby's cooing could do to any surrounding, however desolate it may be.

Most of the hermitage was busy with its morning chores. Healers and disciples had busied themselves with the early morning tasks of watering the plants and inspecting them, selecting only those flowers and fruit and tubers and twigs which were ready to give juices with medicinal properties. Then there was the pruning and weeding out which would take most of the morning.

Amidst all this, they heard a wonderful laughter. All heads turned to see who it was that radiated so much happiness.

They saw her coming down the stone steps from her quarters, holding the baby radiating joy and laughter. All the healers stopped and wondered if one would need medicines if one could laugh like that.

It looked like she had forgotten about her last task. She was immersed in the baby care and had forgotten the world. It was as though all her violent and painful past had been wiped clean with one smile from the baby.

And so, it came to pass. She was at peace and extremely happy to be with baby Nuran. The whole of the hermitage seemed to be rejoicing with the pair. Though they carried out their work with the same zeal and speed, there was a spring in their steps and laughter in their words. A tiny infant had indeed changed the mood of the entire hermitage from a somber and grim environs to a cheery and happy place.

Randolph had had more than one reason to relax. Apart from the mischievous antics of the young child which brought smiles to all, there was also the reassuring news by his confidants who had come back late one night. They had assured the Druid that all was quiet on the borders of the Sabbornese kingdom. Apparently, the neighbors had been quite shaken up with the massacre of the Royals brought in by the golden witch and the disappearance of the Royal heir apparent. These neighboring kingdoms did not wish to invoke the wrath of the golden witch and had decided not to interfere.

There was no movement of any army on the borders. Perhaps, in near future, they may be less tolerant but this was certainly a welcome respite for all in the hermitage.

In the meanwhile, some of the elder citizens of Sabbornes had come together and established an organization to look into the immediate problems of the kingdom. Randolph was more than confident that he could approach them and have peaceful talks.

And, so it came to pass that the mighty rule of the Sabbornese was effectively over, having been routed by a mere whim of a woman. It was almost time for the next harvest to begin. Peace seemed to be returning to the kingdom as people began coming out of their homes; with trepidation earlier but with more confidence, later. Shops and other establishments had begun to open up and the dark memories of that night had become less disturbing. One good outcome of this had been the refusal of the slaves to lead a subhuman existence. The citizens had accepted this and slowly but surely the South Landers were gaining back their space and position in their homeland.

Life at the hermitage had become a smooth affair with Randolph busying himself with his work of brewing a range of healing potions. He had become more cheerful and played with baby Nuran, so christened by Xera in the memory of her long lost brother. Due to a very powerful mixture that Randolph had brewed, the inmates of the hermitage were immune to her deadly charms. For them, she was just Nuran's mother in spite of still being hauntingly beautiful.

On a cool evening, when the sun was casting its last departing golden rays on the hermitage, she had taken baby Nuran to the gardens. The young saplings had grown into luxurious bushes laden with colorful flowers. The fragrance they emitted was heady. Angelica and Suhan, the two healers were picking up some flowers. Both were skilled gardeners and had been phenomenally successful in brewing some special concoctions which healed deep wounds quickly. Randolph had specially instructed them to keep an eye on Xera and the baby. And that is why, they were working near her.

Baby Nuran had just begun to take his first steps and she watched him contentedly. Never had she been so happy and it showed on her beautiful face. The baby was watching a new yellow flower in bloom and it suddenly turned to her and said 'Ma!' Hearing those words, she ran and scooped the baby in her arms. Clinging to it she said loudly, 'I Love you! You are so adorable!'....

It was Angelica who heard the sound first. It was a soft sound of a branch breaking as though some weight had been put on it. She turned and froze. A scream almost escaped her trembling lips. At once she dashed off to library to get her master here. Suhan, turned around and saw the strange spectacle. He moved quickly to the pair and showing a great presence of mind took the falling baby from her hand. But, before he could reach her, she had fallen to the ground with a thud. Making sure that the little one was safe, Suhan turned to her and froze in pure horror. The exquisitely beautiful lady whom he had seen every day was slowly changing into an old, shriveled hag in front of his eyes.

At that precise moment Angelica burst into the garden with Randolph following her. The pair went quickly to Suhan. Randolph made sure that no harm had come to the infant and only then turned his attention to her.

Just a sagging skin and bone now, she was gasping for breath. Her sensuous mouth had turned into a toothless hollow shell and saliva was dripping from it. Her once luminescent eyes, had shrunk into two dark pits and she struggled to look for Randolph.

Realizing what must have happened, Randolph signaled the healers who had followed him to lift her and take her inside. She was put on a soft bed and Randolph sat next to her. 'Master..' her words were a mere whisper and tears ran down on her sunken cheeks. 'Xera.', Randolph called out to her gently and her body was shaken by uncontrollable sobs. He bent down to listen to her knowing that time, indeed was running out for her. She struggled to get up but fell back in his arms. She was searching for someone. Randolph signaled Angelica to bring baby Nuran to him. As Randolph brought the infant closer to her, Xera's face was lit by a smile. She tried to feel his face but her hand went limp. With help from his healers Randolph propped her on few pillows so she could see the baby.

'Do you wish to tell me something, Xera?' Randolph asked her softly.' Is there anything you wish for?' Randolph knew that Xera had executed the plan with great élan and possibly was at peace. Still he wanted to be sure. 'Just one thing'. Xera uttered words, haltingly in the beginning but with clarity and much wisdom as she spoke.' My call has come, O Great Druid. I have but one wish left. Make him a fine man. Teach him to be humble and respectful to all. But most important of all, bring him up not as a Royal but as a commoner.'

As Randolph nodded in affirmation, Xera's head went limp and she closed her eyes. Tears rolling down his eyes, Randolph placed baby Nuran close to her and watched her glide away into the next world. 'Rest well, Xera! You alone knew what true love is...' whispered Randolph.

Xera had accepted the Satanic Chant and lived by its rule. She was at peace, knowing she had accomplished her mission.

Printed by Libri Plureos GmbH in Hamburg,
Germany